How is Travel a Folded Form?

How is Travel a Folded Form?
©2018 Erika Howsare

All rights reserved. No part of this book may be reproduced or transmitted in any form or by any means without written permission of the author.

Saddle Road Press
Hilo, Hawai'i
saddleroadpress.com

Author photograph by Meredith Coe
Book design by Don Mitchell

ISBN 978-0-9969074-6-0

How is Travel a Folded Form?

Erika Howsare

Saddle Road Press

Contents

One   9

Two   33

Three   41

Circle   71

To my parents, the pathmakers

Isabella and I stand in fescue. A sheet of paper lands at our feet.

How is travel a folded form?

I answer:

> "It's been less than two weeks. In that period: homesteading in Whitefish; the gift of a keychain in Buhl, Idaho; Cascades; the Sandpoint beach phone booth; terror in Ellensburg; breakfast in Spokane; joy at Alturas Lake; the Australian who runs the "Impeccably Clean" motel; Shyra and Randy in neo-Nazi territory; road work; Montana mountains; coffee in Missoula; the silly guy in Salmon talking minivans; ski towns and farm towns; a week of rain; perfect Washington farmland; Grand Coulee Dam…."

Isabella answers:

> "This tragic story filled my mind as I rode towards the head of the lake, which became every moment grander and more unutterably lovely."[i]

And then we both say:

> "Half the walk is but retracing our steps."[ii]

Matter: the subject under consideration.

draft author bios — need work

Isabella Bird: English, born 1831. Began traveling in early twenties for her health (she had a "spinal complaint," for which an ocean voyage was the recommended treatment). Became a popular travel writer; was named the first woman Fellow of the Royal Geographic Society. In 1873, after spending time in Hawai'i, she returned to the U.S., set out from San Francisco and made her way east, spending several months in the Plains and Rocky Mountains before returning to England.[iii]

"The wheels made neither sound nor indentation as we drove over the short, dry grass."[iv]

I: Pennsylvanian, born 1977. Began traveling in late teens for recreation and material. In a recent year, she set out from Oakland and made her way east, spending several months in the Plains and Rocky Mountains before returning to Pennsylvania.

"Route 152, 140, 33 again. You could zigzag all over the valley always going north, south, east or west, keeping your bearings by the presence of the hills."[v]

Matter: the events or circumstances of a particular situation.

I grew up with a friend, Laura Ingalls, on paper. PREPARATION. Her westering was as the individual grasshopper, covering fields. She might have rolled, one shoulder then the other, and gotten there as quickly.

But Isabella is my footed analog, closer to my ways and means. She had written: "The air and life are intoxicating. I live mainly out of doors and on horseback, wear my half-threadbare Hawaiian dress, sleep sometimes under the stars on a bed of pine boughs." [v] We will not be pilgrims. I answered: "The sun went down after I ate my avocado and cheese on the bluff, and everything got pink and purple, especially the foam on the water. The trail pushed through the grass, connecting points made of round, pockmarked rocks. I got myself back here in the failing light, feeling strong and pared-down."

Isabella never travels as a group. We face each other, compare contents of bags, wool or acrylic. We have ambitions on blank pages. I vacuumed out the car yesterday; Isabella is sorting through her trunk, piling underwear on one side and gloves on the other. I'll be a fly in a box, smelling one mile for one minute, french fries, ponderosa the tree. Isabella's skirt will fly. One hand on the reins, delicately finding how hooves mean to meadow. She started east (England) of where I (Pennsylvania) began, though we most closely read America facing home.

Eating the last supper, making plans, Isabella wants to know why we all look the same direction and whether those bird sounds are part of the recording or simply occurring. (Like a clear square, the sentence I aspire to.) The recording is salsa music. Neither of us lay any claim to that fact although it makes us eat faster. A readymade reflectiveness. Laura's nose full of grasses' scent, her dress ruined. She recedes from my horizon. I wish I'd ordered the red snapper tacos. We plan our volume: Reverse the primary path. Go east, young women, filling notebooks. Isabella unrolls her napkin.

Line: a wire or pair of wires connecting one telephone with another.

Notes for intro.

"But little time was lost in placing the last spike in position; and it was driven home with a hammer of solid silver in the hands of Stanford, the president of the Central Pacific. Then followed a few addresses, including a prayer, cheers, music and the reading of numerous congratulatory telegrams, which came flashing over the wires from the far east and the far west, as the news of the driving of the last spike spread."[vi]

(from Hittell, "The Continent is Joined")

"Everything suggests a beyond."[vii]

LINE: the gesture of pen on paper; a row of wheat; a stateline; a path, road, river or rut; transubstantiation; latitude and longitude; the railroad; the horizon; the proscenium; the line running directly from silver hammer into telegraph.

— socks
— cooler
— stirrups

Thick old places, to be left. EPISODE. Isabella and I sit on chairs—I think in nearby spots—and read William Darby's description of a dense, early place, written 1782:

> "The site where W——— now stands was a vast thicket of black and red hawthorn, wild plums, hazel bushes, scrub oak, and briars. Often I have picked hazel nuts where the courthouse now stands. The yell of the savage rung in fancy's ear and, alas, too often in the heart of the dying victim. The whole country was a dense forest, only broken by small patches, with dead trees, made so by the axe of the early pioneer."[viii]

Finished is a farm and a wagon road, or a thick and forested past we almost cannot picture. Hazel bushes; house of law; Italian restaurant and a new, Rotarian-donated clock. A long time ago it was already disappearing, thus Darby recorded it and we record our Darby, itchy to retreat. Our destination now is not dense, it's interior. I want to read the younger, thinner places in Isabella's bell-clear sentences.

> "We were running down upon the Great Salt Lake, bounded by the white Wahsatch ranges. Along its shores, by means of irrigation, Mormon industry has compelled the ground to yield fine crops of hay and barley; and we passed several cabins, from which, even at that early hour, Mormons, each with two or three wives, were going forth to their day's work."[ix]

We both think to leave for the newly begun, the caves and canyons, rafting companies, headstrong fences. She could have been my great-great-great-grandmother. We promise each other: *The liminal West makes our making as evident as dirt.* We gouge it. Isabella digs her spurs into the river. Laura howls. Almost drowns. We recall something about "the restoration of a paradisiacal earth."[x] Isabella wants to know when all the screaming got so casual.

Matter: subject of disagreement.

(I'm trying out some headings for these notes)
Premises for Movement

"Creation implies separation."[xi]

Liminal spaces: sunset, nostalgia, stairwell, line break, evaporation, pregnancy, mourning, creole, equal sign, excrement, erosion, conversation

"to 'secure' the snake's head, to drive the peg into it"[xii]

rhyme's gap between sound and sense, midnight, sympathy, eyelid, faultline, the arrow in a chemical reaction, volcano, puberty,

ovulation,

seashore "a most advantageous point from which to contemplate this world"[xiii] (Thoreau)

—We posit no movement is only that.

— what about a title?

Line: something (as a ridge or seam) that is distinct, elongated, and narrow.

Landmarks Sought:

GAPS: The telephone line between two speakers; the caesura in which poetry's "pure word" may be revealed; the rocky space through which a creek drops, its shape manifested as waterfall; the new moon

OVERLAPS: the suburbs; the wetlands; a marriage; the nights of waxing and waning

CRUXES: the continental divide; the highway centerline; the moment when one cell fissures into two; the stroke of midnight ("Every New Year is a resumption of time from the beginning, that is, a repetition of the cosmogony"[xiv]); the moment when the moon is full

OTHER LIMINAL SPACES: Between a photo and the paper it's printed on; between the surface of a mirror and the person looking into it; spaces involving harmonics; several more involving etymology; many involving reading.

By means of irrigation, the paradox of desert as cropland made manifest. By means of travelogue, the paradox of nostalgia for a frontier made manifest. "The 'stranger' unites 'here' and 'there.'"[xv]

Line: a device for catching ghoti*.
* ghoti: fish: [gh] as in *rough*, [o] as in *women*, [ti] as in *description*.

Tires pop some kind of seedpod laying in the street.   EPISODE.   If lines are the first liminality, water is part of what blurs them, as ink faints into paper. "Isabella, are you irrigated?" I want to lie down with her corsets and letters to her sister, her lumpy handwriting that maybe got crossed out, once, by candlelight.

Lacking water, the West loses density. Isabella sees right through it. I'm in the driver's seat. She puts on lipstick in the rearview mirror; she's wearing new boots. Lines all around us: gaps, overlaps, doublings, all thirsty. She reads, "Early settlers were rationed to two hours of water per week for each one-and-one-quarter-acre lot." [xvi] A house nearby is trimmed in marigolds. I straighten my skirt; it's permanent press. Vapor turns into ice. We consider: *Water is always liminal in its presence, absence, cycling, transformation.* A black river draws on white ground.

Other cars approach, retreat; *the river is a gap in the land, an extended line of liminality.* Water trickles down the sidewalk and soaks into the edge where mown lawn meets concrete. Someone's spoon tinkles in a glass. *Line plus water equals bridge.* Isabella will shatter some Englishwoman's parlor, part the waters, dissect the fog. Her neat shelves are tightened. We're almost ready to go.

Line: the course of direction of something in movement; route.

We keep taking notes: *"Metaphor" means bridge.* EPISODE. Late afternoon, Isabella and I get out of the car at the water's edge. *A bridge is a seam.* The orange sign is behind us, up the hill; we decided to ignore it. The little river is flooding. *Or a river is a seam.* Through the young trees, we see the quick dark center of the current, but here where the road just begins to disappear the water is tame and clear. We can't even tell where the usual riverbed might be. *And a bridge is a stitch.* Isabella lies down at the very bottom of the flood, head upstream from feet, so she can breathe. A little foam rides the current. Our car is pulled over with the wheels turned for safety. *Existing on a bridge makes one aware of the shores' interdependence.*[xvii] How long will she breathe down there? Her skirts wave in the flow of runoff, lead, heavy metals, clay, cow manure, chicory ripped off its stems, rusty nails, glass insulators from telephone poles, ear tags from cattle, electric bills, antifreeze, and chicken wire. *They attend or ignore one another.* An old woman drives down the hill; how did she not see the orange sign? *One notes the suspension of one's position.* She smiles as she slides over to the passenger seat, lifting skinny legs and moving foam pillows, so that I can turn her car around for her. Afterward, I look back and Isabella is standing on solid ground again and dry. *Neither east bank nor west; neither water nor soil.* The old woman drives away, still smiling.

Notes on Inscription

An oral epic singer from Tibet named Grags-pa seng-ge who, though illiterate, composes by staring at a blank sheet of paper. S.S.: "It is a bright screen which is part of his singing equipment."[xviii]

(Writing cast in many cultures as an act of literal world-making, enacting and calling forth power, not just recording it. The world in the exchange between the pen and the page; without one, the other cannot exist.)

"By cultivating the desert soil, they in fact repeated the act of the gods, who organized chaos by giving it forms and norms."[xix]

Response to a space seen as empty: inscribe it.

Thinking a sheet of paper was blank, we wrote our names on it. The desert was empty of water; they irrigated it, writing long rows of alfalfa and corn. Thinking the West was empty of civilization, they freely deeded the land to any willing settler, including some whose role was to plant trees in order to make the plains look more like the Eastern forests. Out there, west of Salt Lake City, people spell their names in rocks on the moist white salt flats called Bonneville.

— could be a way to organize chapters?

Line: a horizontal row of written or printed characters.

Shivering, Isabella and I dip water with tin cups. EPISODE. She clears her throat and makes a note about engines. A woman with half-closed eyes and a fitted cap wanders past. Trees are deciding how they want things to go. The gravelly water stains our sleeves. Isabella wipes her forehead with a wet hand, leaves streaks in mud; all around her as she straightens up are falling leaves and twisted scraps of paper, describing air currents.

Wrapping wool around our bodies, we look backwards at our own path, which ends under our feet. We take to it like ants following a chemical trace. Isabella looks out from the passenger side and sees single trees with scenery rotating behind them, trees with space to grow and fall over, leaves sifted at their feet. Everything is damp after the storm, lights are blinking through screens, soft sounds of typing fill the car. We wind off to the north, tapping our feet.

~~Guidebook to Modern American Travel~~

I don't like this; much too grandiose

Notes on Description

(Writing as a distillation, a means of transmitting experience from one person to another, an aid to memory. The page as false cognate for passive container. The pen as technology enabling preservation of what is valued.)

"Leave no trace. Stick to well-worn, hard-packed trails and forest roads whenever possible."[xx]

(from V. guidebook)

Response to a place seen as full: describe it.

The place, the destination, surrounds the traveler and enfolds the senses with what is unfamiliar. The traveler thinks she is more likely to be changed than is her destination, for example, when visiting a national park. She frames little bits of the environment in her camera's viewfinder, chooses elements to reproduce in postcard messages, allows parts to stand for whole. This edifies her.

"To follow a road is to accept an interpretation."[xxi]

Line: a state of order, control, or obedience.

Isabella and I are always on bridges, even when everything is dry. Episode. We drive past the factory-cum-brewery, the little post office, the straight part of the route with a railroad on one side and Calf Mountain ahead, books on the floor of the car, plastic soldier on the dashboard. We imagine living here and there. You put in a driveway or you just paint. One slope is covered in knee-high plants turning red. One cowers below electric lines and high towers.

She writes about where she wants to picnic and ride, then I write about her horse. She writes a memory:

> "This man, known through the Territories and beyond them as 'Rocky Mountain Jim,' or more briefly, as 'Mountain Jim,' is one of the famous scouts of the Plains, and is the original of some daring portraits in fiction concerning Indian Frontier warfare...He is a man for whom there is now no room, for the time for blows and blood in this part of Colorado is past..."[xxii]

I watch a Mountain Jim show from the driver's seat. Things have gotten taller, I tell her. I write,

> "I went off to look for a trailhead which the info board at the campground had mentioned on its cheery Things-To-Do list, but it proved elusive amongst the cows and tall grasses. A ranger told me it hadn't been maintained so she wouldn't even try to explain where it used to be."

Something to add to our notes: *Myths preceded wagon ruts onto the plains.* You can still follow deer and rabbit trails, I tell her. She picks her favorite of my sentences.

We stand openmouthed at a chasm of air where dry leaves blow like flecks of gold. Isabella proves to me thus that land exists. She wants to know how anklebones lead to six-packs, how Vespas lead to myocardial infarction, how the Sunday paper leads to sugar packets, how salads lead to antique furniture. *When a frontier is visible, so is its legend, and its advertising.* I point out signs to her, and which ones are worth saving.

> Let's skip the title discussion for now
> and just keep gathering...
> Notes on the Refraction of the Line

A trespass is a liminal space between law and chaos.

To correct the emptiness of the desert or plains, you make things grow. To correct the fullness of forest, you cut things down.

A person who navigates a city on foot will conceive of the street as a negative space and the curb as a positive space: when she steps from the crosswalk onto the safer sidewalk, she is encountering a place of relevance to her. Nearby, a person driving through the city sees the same corner in the opposite way, where the street is the positive (navigable) space, and the sidewalk is off-limits. The city is full of these opposing worldviews, brushing one another's skins.

L.L.: "Unfenced land is now rare. In free range areas, non-ranching landowners must fence livestock *out*."[xxiii]

The first frost arrives when descriptions inscribe their subjects.

How is Travel a Folded Form?

This is why our muscles are tired—from holding up a hill's worth of houses. EPISODE. Isabella and I arrive at an endpoint, having traveled a spoke to center. Curve to the left, there's a subdivision. To the right, an unused paddock. I make a note: *The boundary between arable and not, liveable and not, has historically been mobile.* The endpoint has mounted an exhibition, shelves and shelves of outdated photos: the Northern Pacific Railway under construction, the new towns it created, Yellowstone with its images printed on coasters and dusted once a week all over the world. Isabella leads me into the Old Faithful Inn, venerable treehouse, rough-hewn diagonals, burlwood columns, stair treads made of half a log. To be ripe is so much more the other side of eating paper. *A visible, living frontier was already underlain by its own rapidly expanding mythology.*

Isabella and I sit at art-deco writing desks on the mezzanine and write postcards under green-shaded lamps. We stricture ourselves, we lose momentum, we finish our thoughts. We go downstairs where friendly teenagers from all over the United States are serving dinner. (We get Shea, from Alabama.) Isabella wants to know how we could be so fertile. Or prone to curling at the edges, yellowing. Shea sets down white cups and saucers, stubby fingers on souvenir spoons, patting the apron at her hips. Complex arrangements of fabric and stem, we. In two dimensions we indescribably palpate, present ourselves outward, write "green lamps—bison—the geyser not spotlit at night so a splash in the dark—flag in the crow's nest—" Entirely possible just to dust ourselves away, except for all our plastic parts. I once read somewhere, *Humans think about sensation far better than we sensate in the first place.*

Outside, a bison is aligned with the geyser in the blackness, nearly invisible. Isabella and I go back to our Frontier Cabin, thinking of eruptions nobody watches, in midwinter.

Matter: substance of which a physical object is composed.

Landscape Comparison Charts (LCCs)

Arcadia: shepherds tend their flocks
in a unchanging, circular way of life
that resembles sleepwalking.

                              Utopia: "It was a military post, but at present
                              consists of a few frame houses put down
                              recently on the bare and burning plain.
                         ...These new settlements are altogether revolting,
                     entirely utilitarian, given up to talk of dollars as well
                                          as to making them."[xxiv]

In order to build the city, one must
enter the countryside;

                              in order to create fullness, one must
                                      start with what is empty.

Drudgery ensues.

                                  Solnit: "If the work of making is
                                      predicated on absence,

...the labor of tending is organized
around presences (tending maintains
the products of work)."[xxiv]

                            Underlying and enabling Utopia's
                  noble one-off projects—the construction
                          of the railroad, the dramatic rushes
                onto newly appropriated chunks of land—

were the same simple, repetitive tasks
that people had done and were still

doing back East and everywhere.
Much of this labor was assigned to
women: mending clothes, building
fires, sweeping dirt floors.

                      Though the bold and dangerous
                  journeys of pioneers garner much
                                of our remembrance,

the years after arrival constituted
most of the real stuff of pioneering—that is,

                                      walking
soon became sleepwalking—that is,

                    the wide movements of wide-awake
                                      inscription

were supported by cyclical labor
like wheels rolling under a wagon.

Line: a general plan.

Isabella and I watch a parade. EPISODE. We're sitting in a hot spot, backs to the wall, noticing pairs of people who look alike. Two men with short hair. Two girls wearing tights. One person singing about his lost love, Prudence. She writes: "They wear boots, but never two of one pair, and never blacked, of course, but no stockings..."[xxv] Some of the parade-goers wear feathers in their caps and some are tracking the weather on handheld devices. Horses snort as they round the corner. A guitar player marches past us in buckskins, then a clown on stilts reciting cowboy poetry. Pant legs riffle in the breeze; children squint at pies behind Main Street shop windows. They're wearing pink jackets. The antibacterial soap in the public library restroom is almost gone, warns the lady next to us. Isabella writes, "Work, work, work is their day and their life."[xxvi] How old is that woman with the white-blonde hair? The front of the parade catches up with the back. She rubs her fingers together absently. Everyone around us is carrying an insurance card with their eyes protected by mirrored shades. Isabella wants to know when the sidewalks became so dense. I remember reading: "A yoke was made to place across the shoulders, so as to carry at each end a bucket of water, and then water was brought a half mile from spring to house."[xxvii] Six model homes go by on floats with plastic FOR SALE signs stuck in their false front yards.

Circle: to move or revolve around.

LCCs, cont'd.
(these are on the long side, but I think that's OK, even normal)

"He would be a poet who...transplanted
[words] to his page with earth adhering
to their roots." (T.) xxviii

                              The metaphors that drove manifest destiny
                                   gave pioneering its meaning, but

so did the literal dirty work of pioneering
life. Pioneering was an inescapably
grounded experience

                        driven by an ethos which explicitly struggles
                                to overcome the particularities
                                          of the ground.

"If dirt has meaning, then meaning is
everywhere." (S.) xxix

                                       When we invent a word,
                                     we make a new territory;

The new world quickly sets about
layering itself, describing and evolving,
traveling through and around itself in
circular patterns, a single word accreting
multiple meanings—

a new shoe collecting dirt.

Line: source of information; insight.

Isabella, though well-off, is waiting for the weather to break.   EPISODE. We drive past a sound barrier protecting houses that are separated by flags. Every blade of grass is a universe and an asset. On the horizon a bruise-colored ridge slides behind creamy houses. She writes: "The absence of a date shows my predicament. *They* have no newspaper; *I* have no almanack...This is 'a life in which nothing happens.'"[xxx] Upstairs windows look down to avoid each other's gazes. Children lie on carpets wearing socks. Isabella says she needs to wash her face. The highway is so wide, a separate formation just over or under the surface of the ground, seen as broad because we nearly recline as we skim it. Or it is a room whose walls are trees and can be passed through. Sheds, creeks and the backs of sheds mark points in the field that pass at constant speed.

We're drawing an arc. A long ridge repeatedly turns us away. Isabella would like to feel warm water on her face. Houses disappear as we move past taller hills or humps of ground where the highway cuts in. She smooths her skirt. Each day we've marked our progress—twice, three times. A shaking tree looms, recedes. What does that house remind her of? A child, picking at carpet pile, lying on her stomach after supper. An angled sky opens when we emerge from one radio band. We remember our favorite books. I remind her of this: "I sat down and knitted for some time—my usual resource under discouraging circumstances...A distressed emigrant woman has just given birth to a child in a temporary shanty by the river, and I go to help her each day."[xxxi] A fear of losing our houses behind a mountain, or losing our way within ridges. She rubs her face with strong hands.

Circle: to enclose in or as if in a circle.

More LCCs

Remove playbook from sleeve.

All European settlers in the West had some idea of what they were getting into, because they had heard or read accounts from previous adventurers.

"Geotagging Uses G.P.S. Technology to Organize Photos and Show the World Where You've Been."[xxxii] (NYT)

If all travel is, in that sense, travelogue,

all travelogue is ekphrasis.

Open playbook to instructions page.

The description is both a window that allows us to see where we are going,

and a mirror that reflects us back to ourselves as we move.

Dirt will cloud them.

"Pick the museums you would like to visit and schedule your time wisely."[xxxiii]

Line: chronological series.

Isabella wants to know about the planting of ornamental grasses in grid patterns on gas station lawns. EPISODE. We wander around the circular campground road, looking at exhibits. At the feet of the woods, small crinkled movements. Little figures hunch under awnings, as still as fired clay. A ranger gives us stickers to pin on our shoulders. One dog stands at attention on the end of a red leash. Someone exits an RV, the narrow screen door hissing shut behind him, a tray of toasted buns in his hand. Our feet find the edge of the state-issued pavement, where leaves and gravel begin, and I switch on a flashlight attached to my forehead in order to read: "At the creek camp, water continually dripped into the tents and brush shelters, putting out fires that were intended to keep the occupants warm." [xxxiv]

The year plunges downward, increasing the bass-note blare of altitude. We know some roads will soon become like dark closets. We look around for similar animals, unwilling to be like thoughtless wolves, shivering with instinct. *On this spot an encampment of emigrants endured ten days of unseasonable freezing conditions.* Snow would collect in our tails. We heat a can of soup on a propane stove and eat it for dinner along with sliced cheddar. We're good at unrolling our sleeping bags in a minute or less, but one tent pole is patched ineffectively with duct tape. Near the restroom building, a small constant sound means a water heater running, and a diagonal path cutting off a corner. Or would we cease to exist, like frogs before the thaw?

An old woman wearing a horse T-shirt bends further and further toward a quarter on the dirt. Isabella writes, somewhat wistfully, "A solitary hunter has built a log cabin up here, which he occupies for a few weeks for the purpose of elk-hunting, but all the region is unsurveyed, and mostly unexplored."[xxxv] We brush crumbs, spread our atlas on the picnic table, look on the maps for areas of green and their flocks of little triangles. These are places to sit and to sleep, meaning tents. Dotted lines connect us. A sign at the road's bend explains the two types of arrowheads found nearby. We don't stay up long after dark.

How is Travel a Folded Form?

> Last of the LCCs
> (I think— and let's please find a better name for them)

                      A drawstring bag, a marketing plan, a
                      path with a railing. Everything significant
                      must have a name. So must everything
              that is for sale, everything that is to be proven.

H: "which does not consist in a clutching
or any other kind of grasping, but rather
in a letting come of what has been dealt out"[xxxvi]

                      "Gold is pure; dirt is what is eliminated
                      along the way."[xxxvii]

"A cattleman dug up some wild onions
for a snack

                      and found gold flakes attached
                      to their roots." [xxxviii]

                      Names of towns: Oro Valley, Orofino,
                      Orogrande, Oroville, Goldfield, Gold Point,
            Golden Gate, Golden State, Silver City, Silver Springs,
              Silverton, Silver State, Silver Peak, Copper Canyon,
                Copper Mountain, Eureka, Rico, Eldorado,
                    Paradise, Paradise Valley, Point Sublime,
                            Diamond Mountains,
                                  Paradox.

Advanced move:
To travel without names.
To relish the taste.

On the line: in complete commitment and at great risk.

[From the second Chapter of the Guidebook to Modern American Travel.]

Notes on Ambivalence

these are of course the notes from when we were apart

Would it be a line	Split, a language
Would the line V	saying paradox
As such emergence	Of clearing as in pushing
it will fold	on plants from the center
on itself	The movement
V, cotyledon	will not be prised from its tools
From it issues	Its boots
infant, issues speech,	The perfect being
the open mouth	bisected
like an atom splitting	"So is all art form
shaped on a system	of oppositions, balance
without parity	what we mean by composition
in art is simply right	and left
handed	ness, one hand and
a pot	hook." (M. Austin.) [lxvi]

All the West becomes a reflection	When the frontier closes
in 1891	in 1891
when the frontier closes	all the West becomes a reflection

Isabella writes: "By evening we were running across the continent on a bee line, and I sat for an hour on the rear platform of the rear car to enjoy the wonderful beauty of the sunset and the atmosphere...The bright metal track, purpling like all else in the cool distance, was all that linked one with Eastern or Western civilization."[xxxix] EPISODE.   She longs for the garden. I go on foot. She rode horseback to the station.

My map, do not trespass, the road is a container. She enters it and slaps reins; one path is the first. This is translation. The trip sinks into the ground. The road reiterates. Hovers, a bridge: the body longs, it moves, a mirror suspended. It finds a path and gives the horse its head. It means to be seamless as in border around and can be counted as positive or negative space, and understood if you are crossing the street or getting up from your chair. Any position has at least two sides, but it is still a point. And if river was the first road, what meant the bridge.

Isabella determines by looking into the cleft of the railroad that she and I should split up. We will write each other postcards at appointed times. Reception will be difficult.

Reflect: to turn into or away from a course: deflect.

Isabella goes off to study photographs. First she wants to learn how to see in frames. She takes notes:

> William Henry Fox Talbot's *Articles of Glass*, a salt print from a paper negative, 1844, three shelves with 19 glasses and champagne flutes and pitchers and decanters, arranged symmetrically. Containers, empty, three-dimensional, hover against a velvet darkness, their roundness limned by suggestive curves and grooves.

I write to her:

> I feel larger in my body now, but smaller in my mouth. I am rushing out even in sleep. I want my own square mile. My legs go wider forward to bite off the grass. These plains are so thin and delicious, gulpable, stretchable, my arms are the only arms, unopposed. I am making my own alphabet, I'm speeding over billions. Haven't been seen in a week. Have grown by thirds. The compass throws its darts out from my palm and I am unpierced, just under clouds. I understand everything now and there is no one to explain it to. This is fully interior, Isabella, do you know that? And I am being drawn out by gas pedals, bootheels, fingers.
>
> I am leaving, leaving, leaving—a little volume smeared over states and then more flat states. My body metal and moving.

Do you know what approaches?

Matter: formless substratum of all things which exists only potentially and upon which form acts to produce realities.

How is Travel a Folded Form?

I don't entirely remember whose notes are whose...
(by the way, have you seen my keys?...)

        Painting is a window: The frame on the view
           A photo is a mirror

          Glass is a machine   Is a map
              Land is round,   Projected on a grid, land
       but a single cool eye   as if Xeroxed
                   unearned

      Stand in a high place   Bluff or cliff
    A crux of sky and ground   static as paint:
        A view rolls down,   fields, or roads.
then this texture, this slope,   What supports the feet is
        exact and particular   damp moment in flux.
              like a photo   Old maps show buildings
                   As 3D   and a horizon
                as if a bird   looking from a high point
         had drawn the map   figures and animals near rivers.
    Yet streets are labeled as   all is openly as
                  if known   unlike the seated painter

Something is currently writing   with yellowed accounts
                like a window   or a mirror
                firmly placed   in a sentence

Next Isabella wants to learn why things are gathered inside, just so. She takes notes:

> Eugène Atget, 1926-27, *Magasins du Bon Marché*. The photograph presents glass as both window and mirror. Five mannequins behind a shop window, wearing long coats and hats, their gazes thrown in all directions. They stand on a stage, among opposing objects, indifferent and hidden. Their faces or feet are occluded by furniture and especially by the window's reflection of the Paris street: tall buildings, balconies, more windows. Is Atget himself in the reflection? No, he has taken a diagonal stance that strikes his own figure from the image. Yet his rectangular frame gathers the floating planes, the slow, silent chaos, the lonely, diagonal gazes into something ordered and honest. Everything stands still inside the corners. Silver print from glass negative.

I write to her:

> I remember that from some curves in the road you could see the city in its shimmering grid, and the desert mountains on the west side. I set up my tent and took a walk over to the grove, open-mouthed from disconnectedness, not awe. The signage broke my eye. Everything you can touch is smoothed and oiled by so many hands before. There it was, in its actuality, smaller than I imagined. And I keep looking at everything from the wrong angle. My mood is flattened by this sense of seeing myself in a tree or splayed over a fence. Brought to knees by sense of not seeing properly; I assume things exist, though they are not always visible. Still I look right at them, such a coveted chance, and my gaze goes right through and on to a pair of shorts or a used ice cream dish. The open lines I was licking have fractured, decayed.
>
> P.S. Send field glasses. Would like to become a birder.

Reflect: to give back or exhibit as an image, likeness, or outline: mirror.

How is Travel a Folded Form?

        The legend of   Tornado Alley
            a favorite   does not guarantee
  made of hard roads   a sighting
  and white-on-green   except
             machines   of itself

Reflect: to have a bearing or influence.

Isabella takes notes on why boxes are inviting.

> Timothy O'Sullivan, *Black Cañon, Colorado River, Looking Below from Big Horn Camp*, 1871. The Colorado a perfect mirror for vertical walls of dark rock. The weighty cliffs are forbidding and of uncertain scale, but we float at the level of the water's surface, seeing from a human point of view. No figures are present; only raw water and rock. One imagines oneself bursting through a screen, enfolding this emptiness.
>
> Tomorrow I study stereoscopes.

Do you know what aligns in such a pattern?

I write to her:

> I feel the grass being knit together with a thin blue line across my forehead. Places I've never or seldom seen are seared in my shoulders. You might have sniffed a breath to locate us, and now I keep the numbers taped to my wrist. I rub my face on my atlas, wanting to break into the paper, inhabit the cool greens and blues. Can you remember the bend in the Yellowstone River where we watched the girls hop the gully? Isabella, I not only recall it, I put it between my hands as I fall asleep. Every night I understand better: first up, then across, ten switchbacks to a meadow. I savor the metallic taste of this arrogance. You might have hearsay and a horse. I have invisible nets on my hands. It pulls, it pulls, it pulls us together. I feel a settlement as though I see the future. Get back, and we will reach an end.

Line: to come into the correct relative position.

How is Travel a Folded Form?

What do you think about a "Reader Questionnaire?"
(Would need some instructions, i.e.
"Please get a pen or sharp pencil, then answer the following...
Go on!...")

Number of states visited in your lifetime:_____

Body height:_____

Greatest distance traveled in one day:_____

Fondest out-of-state memory: _____

Best advice received from a stranger:_____

Average walking speed: _____

Preference: _____ metal _____soil

Present location: _____

Most salient daily landmark: _____

Years at current residence: _____

Year, make and model: _____

Feelings about flat land: _____

Preference: _____ Internet _____ trains

Number of species you can identify: _____

Best sentence ever composed: _____

Favorite brochure ever discarded: _____

Are you a photographer? _____ yes _____ always

Field: _____

Favorite constellation: _____

Form: the component of a thing that determines its kind.

> Notes on a Stable Relation
> (Maybe we could have some sort of graphic of a triangle on this page?)

"The human body is blind except for the minute exception of the eyes." (Swensen.)[xl]

> "By this fluctuation the pond asserts its title to a *shore*, and thus the shore is *shorn*, and the trees cannot hold it by right of possession….It licks its chaps from time to time." (Thoreau.)[xli]

>> "Before the tradition of oil painting, medieval painters often used gold-leaf in their pictures. Later gold disappeared from paintings and was only used for their frames. Yet many oil paintings were themselves simple demonstrations of what gold or money could buy. Merchandise became the actual subject-matter of works of art." (Berger.)[xlii]

>> "I watch the passage of the morning [train] cars with the same feeling that I do the rising of the sun, which is hardly more regular." (Thoreau.)[xliii]

"Landscape is light alone." (Swensen.)[xliv]

Matter: to be of importance; signify.

We are all three in the same place at different times. LOCATION. It is a lake called T———. You, I and Isabella, each of us alone, are standing on the shore. Pebbles roll below our feet and shadows of birds roll over pebbles. Arms of pines reach and reach. Isabella takes notes: "The air is keen and elastic. There is no sound but the distant and slightly musical ring of the lumberer's axe."[xlv] I say to myself, "Another notch on the belt of the trip. T—— by full moon, lots of lake shimmering back at the sky. To see it from a plane on a night like this!"

The lake is enormous: a deep, gothic state of its own, a corner of swirling motion within rock and trajectory. You are underneath a little tree. You remember triangulation: To fix your location, you stand and look at two points and you notice what falls in line with these. In one direction, a rock behind a stump; in another, a blinking tower behind a cabin. This is nothing that wasn't already there. There is enough of what is. There is already shape; now you know its edges. Gently, the lake talks back on its molasses skin.

In slowing, we constellate. Or one point draws away from the other two, lengthening the shape. By twos, we flick our tails and observe a third. For each pair of us the third is a landmark: a monument or rift. Isabella draws a map in her small book with links and names, the turn in the road, the origin of drainage, the three o'clock office with linoleum floor. I scratch in the little sandy beach: "Any intersection of longitude and latitude can become a city. A triangle is a very stable shape for building." What are you photographing? The natural clearing called *lake*?

We meet then on a dock, all three of us, and declare that the stasis of landmark is a fruitless gesture and a repetition of the deceased. The continent is untranslatable. What if all were mapped—where would the bottom be let to fall out? In wandering, naming speeds up and roughens the seam. We temporarily look in one another's faces, in order to compose a manifesto.

> *Matter*: *Christian Science:* the illusion that the objects perceived by the physical senses have the reality of substance.

> here's what I want to use as the Intro to the Manifesto, by all three of us

Case study at Yellowstone National Park: A grizzly bear devours a bison in the middle of a river.

The road full of onlookers, parked willy-nilly, binoculars and telephotos trained on the sight. This morning, after the good night's sleep in the hotel, but before the breakfast too big to finish: the elderly filing toward their waiting bus, all sun-hatted and walking-shoe-shod, the smell of diesel in the parking lot. In the lobby are kids in new ten-gallons. In the town square are arches made of antlers, plate glass full of Westernwear. The surroundings are a prairie of working ranches, a valley full of nothing but fence, green grass, spraying irrigators, and sunlight; then a magnetism draws one up the street toward the Gap, into the restaurants, the last-chance gas stations, then into Grand Teton with its neatly separated stops, then up the lonely well-traveled road to Yellowstone, through the entry gates to verify parks pass, on to stops at this and that Visitor Center, and finally the grand encounter. It's a particular movie. The audience chats about sitting, standing, and ambling bison; elk; fumaroles; rivers and lakes; 14,000-foot peaks; a 1,500-foot canyon; burned lodgepole forests; mudpots; their impractical shoes. Invisible lines extend from camera lenses—dotted lines, marking distance.

Manifesto

Cotyledal is a brand-new word. Our directions: how the map lost its border; how the ubiquitous frightens the edge. Proscenium. Harvest. The measure. How atmosphere gradually fades. Flame and seeds both are periphery.

The triangle is stable when it sits on its bottom. When the river blends into ocean it also causes land to blend with water, depositing silt. Delta means change. The triangle teeters on one point, lands heavily. Lands like a body. A spreading mouth.

Icarus overreaches the unmeasured and so does the atlas or the pointing finger. Deltoid is a "triangular muscle that covers the shoulder joint and serves to raise the arm laterally" and delta wing is a "triangular swept-back airplane wing with straight trailing edge".

Thus, we hereby identify muscle, silt and jet. We hereby pluck the triangular constellation's three corners out, each to its own, in lonely jars. We hereby topple the landmark and halt the treading thereupon; we splash water on these three—*Body, Land and Machine*—so as to check for temperature.

We hereby declare ourselves lost.

Circle: a curving side street.

You and Isabella and I feel a duty, threefold, toward representation. (Do we not?) ASSIGNMENTS. So we take sides—or corners, rather. Do you want Body? We do not know you well. I am interested in bones, and the biology of watching state lines flash past. Equine footsteps paper my sleep. But I will take Machine if you like, despite my suspicion of prosthetics and ownership generally. I've seen you with your camera; perhaps you want to take your film in, draw heavy marker lines on prints or trainsounds, make some calls.

Do not take this as offense. Isabella hastens to declare an affinity with flesh (shivering, she says she needs water before it gets dark) and this puts me in mind of a hill I knew, back on the coast, a great hump of lifted fossils that tumbled me down between its flanks to hear the threaded calls of migrators in winter. So I will take Land, unless you'd rather. Isabella is already thumbing the shoulder joints of passersby and blinking back sweat. I'm halfway onto the grass. You do own a compass, yes? You've driven to town? Your route is quite regular. I'll take Land, then. Reader, you take Machine. Isabella, the Body, eyes you with unease.

Form: conduct regulated by extraneous controls (as of custom or etiquette).

How is Travel a Folded Form?

Notes on Relations of Body and Machine

One watches the necessary fact of distance collapse into a simple abstraction of iron; one feels the measure of distance stutter. Societies slip between modes of movement.

Exhibit A:

Variable footsteps are replaced by the regularity of railroad ties. The fingerprint grain of trees sawed and planed into predictable shapes, laid like a series of leapfrogging equal signs below the rails.

Exhibit B:

The train between Truckee and Cheyenne had sleeping berths with fine linen sheets and was "carefully kept at 70°", though "it was 29° outside." [xlvi]

Exhibit C:

Exhibit D:

The car fragments the body by centering its power in the hands and feet, while keeping the legs and arms relatively inactive. Sight is mirrored, the eyes scanning a field that includes views of the future and the past, but not of the present (other cars enter our mirrors' blind spots when they are closest to us, most closely aligned with our own present position). The hood becomes our horizon and the car's frame the boundary of our small, self-contained country.

Exhibit E:

"The rhythm of walking [is] always a recognizable background for our thoughts, altered from the militaristic stride to the jog of the wide, unrutted earth."[xlvii] (M.A.) "In a sense the car has become a prosthetic."[xlviii] (R.S.)

Exhibit F:

"The interstate is its own song. From our hotel room, a room with a balcony you can't access in a box between two freeways and an airport, I saw the sun shining on traffic, green signs, and mountains off somewhere with their angular horizon lines darker than the shimmering heat of the valley floor. This too is home: the coast-to-coast powerlines, cities in an extreme lengthwise shape with their own culture and laws. The mitigated views, reductive services."

Exhibit G:

Line: a glib often persuasive way of talking.

How is Travel a Folded Form?

As an experiment, you and Isabella, Machine and Body, set out for town. EPISODE. She plods along, tumbles downhill, runs her hand through her sun-warmed hair. Meanwhile you surge and shimmy, taut on your axles. You would like to reach: _____ tonight. You miss: _____fiercely, like broken pistons. She counts *caws* as she goes and likens them to heartbeats, though the crows are more like a small tornado over the field. Clouds' shadows slide along, swallowing fenceposts and gas stations, then releasing them to the loudness of full sun. She writes, "There were wonderful ascents then up which I led my horse; wild fantastic views opening up continually, a recurrence of surprises; the air keener and purer with every mile, the sensation of loneliness more singular."[xlix] An insect sounds like a bicycle. You say, as machine, you're tired of following Isabella's soft wandering, but she doesn't hear you because she's listening to the slow statement of a hammer on a beam. You cannot agree on a pace. The wind looms up into many lines. One blue one reclines the horizon, not a river or a road, just the presence of distance. You would like to get to it by: _____. You switch on the: _____. Then you sing along.

Line: a mark as by pencil that forms part of the formal design of a picture distinguished from the shading or color.

Exhibit H:

Exhibit I:

I-80: The prefix "I" as singular self, as I-beam for building. To travel one road thinking of another. To walk on Friday and think of Thursday. By "north" to mean "up". If speed could be measured by stopping for an instant.

Exhibit J:

The body prepares the way for the machine. When you choose a route you describe the land. When you walk on snow or through tall grass, your description makes a path and your choice inscribes the field. A field is a language; a choice within it is a particularity of phrase. Once it has been chosen, it stands as inscription.

Exhibit K:

Berry: "[A path] is a form of contact with a known landscape....[A road's] wish is to avoid contact with the landscape...its aspiration, as we see clearly in the example of our modern freeways, is to be a bridge."[i]

Exhibit L:

Every aphorism and canonical poem starts as a chosen possibility in one speaker's mind. Animal paths become footpaths, then trappers' routes, then wagon roads, then routes for cars and semi trucks. By this time they inscribe the bodies who travel them.

Exhibit M:

Spotted, 2:35 pm: An RV with model name *The Intruder*.

Exhibit N:

"I cannot describe my feelings on this ride, produced by the utter loneliness, the silence and dumbness of all things, the snow falling quietly without wind, the obliterated mountains, the darkness, the intense cold, and the unusual and appalling aspect of nature. All life was in a shroud, all work and travel suspended. There was not a foot-mark or wheel-mark. There was nothing to be afraid of."[ii]

Reflect: to throw back light or sound.

It is a difficult trip the two of you are having. EPISODE. You're sitting on folding chairs, taking in a view. According to reports, a spackling of birdsound could be fighting words. You pull out your reference books, linking the eye-of-the-tree with an experience of seeing. No one covers the heightened sound of swelled creeks like two bridges, one northbound, one broken. Your categories push their conventions into one another's teeth. Isabella meanwhile writes absentmindedly by letting wind blow the paper against her uncapped pen. The sun returns. A jay and some crows do what they were born to do. She thinks she hears, quite unseasonably, an unfrozen frog. You're gazing at the place where a roll of wire fencing must have run out and been grafted to another. "This takes hands," you say defensively. She upsets you when she peers at her own skin.

The two of you, on the way to this hilltop, developed a list of vague resolutions. Yours was to _____ more carefully, with an eye toward historical correctness. Hers was to smell everything more deeply. When you look into the sun you see fuzzy white seeds floating swiftly here and there, and you extrapolate how many there must be on all sides, for the most part invisible. Perhaps they could be netted. Your mind wanders back to the map, the series of routes to get to _____: Route ____, Route ____, and _____ Road. Isabella is talking about how she misses _____. The food, she explains, was to die for.

A mile away, a large gun fires five times, its sound ballooning toward you. You feel like gathering all these people, the county's thin population and its thousands of intentions, in some kind of net, like the floating seeds, and sticking them carefully to the inside walls of a tall, square box. You feel like moving her through many places in a short time, watching her erode.

I send the two of you a postcard:

> Craters of the Moon, Idaho: Camped between outcrops of the porous, jagged black rock that covers the area, except for some sage, a brave little wildflower with white leaves and pink blooms, and pine trees marked by a parasitic mistletoe which secretes growth hormone and causes the tree to grow the affected branch into a frenzy of twigs called a witches' broom. Has the same grotesque appeal as a hand with more than five fingers. Mountains of lava, jagged fields, acres of round, swirling shapes that make the lava's flow exactly obvious. An explorer as late as 1920 got stuck for lack of water and—horrifying—no level ground to sleep on. Now there is a paved path and one is not permitted to stray, for preservation's sake. I drove into the campground through a Do Not Enter and was instantly pulled over by a ranger.

Circle: a territorial or administrative division or district.

Exhibit O:

"Pilgrimage walks a delicate line between the spiritual and the material in its emphasis on the story and its setting."[lii]

Exhibit P:

Travel is a maze; tourism is a labyrinth. We are in a narrow chute, waiting in line and wearing down the path. The higher goal will not be achieved unless the body completes its task. Do not cut across concentric pathways.

Exhibit Q:

Exhibit R:

Inscription can mean permission for pilgrims to follow the pioneer; for the pioneer herself, a track laid down may be the ruination of what had been pure. Corollary: Once the mark has been made, a new page must be sought.

Exhibit S:

Poetry slows time.

Exhibit T:

In travel, the glass of tourism roughens and becomes more like a mirror than a window, reflecting us back to ourselves through a medium of changing surroundings.

Exhibit U:

"We see the movement not the images."

Exhibit V:

Exhibit W:

Poetry clouds the glass of prose.

Exhibit X:

Thoreau again: "Unto a life which I call natural I would gladly follow even a will-o'-the-wisp through bogs and sloughs unimaginable, but no moon nor firefly has shown me the causeway to it."[liii]

Exhibit Y:

"Woolly feelings and ideas are clarified in the presence of objective images."[liv] (Tuan) "How far to the next thing?" the hikers asked.

Exhibit Z:

"Places that declare themselves to be *somewhere* perversely make me feel I am *nowhere*."

Now it's raining lightly on a river of birds. Episode. Thunder of takeoff, wheeling, pouring—they compete with two planes, first a commuter then a fighter. You think their sound is like numbers, Isabella hears cells. Water on the blades and on the larger, louder individuals. The field is busted. This force streams up at you: thousands and thousands of whistles, a steady run that grows blacker, birds chipping off as leaves and zipping or dropping to ground, sometimes a minor lace of them floating off above where more are drifted on the grass. Tens of thousands pour past you; trees regain foliage made of birds. Birds show dimensions by the hundreds of feet in their movements. You listen for the starling's telltale wolf whistle as in your guide, but it is not in evidence or perhaps just obscured by its numeracy. Isabella's eyes are peeled. The hill is a theater and you are on the proscenium and birds are the hall. They say they are arrived; they call something vanquished. *Red-winged blackbird: Flocks of up to 100,000 have been reported.*

Form: a body (as of a person): figure.

Reader, Machine, you have been leaving gaps where there might be feeling, a cold sort of listening. DIFFICULT TALK. You are measuring this and that but Isabella and I are truly asking for your marks, your actual manifested self in sentence. (For fairness' sake, you understand.) Whatever was seeded in your survey, it has not yet fully come—so to speak—to fruit. And of course there was the time you _____ .

Perhaps you are tired, or unoiled.

Isabella and I are not insensitive; in fact sensitivity is our entirety. We are sprawled in the front seats, struggling to roll down the windows. It's too hot for an argument. We will let you rest as needed. Do not miss us or worry: We have been traveling alone together for a long time.

Form: a mold in which concrete is placed to set.

How is Travel a Folded Form?

Notes on Relations of Body and Land

A guide moves herself a long way through a canyon using a lever. "Nancy Kelsey, barefoot to relieve her blisters, carried Ann in her arms while leading her horse down the stony mountainsides…When they broke into the San Joaquin Valley, they found an abundance of fowl, deer, antelope and, said Dawson, 'the most delicious grapes I had ever eaten.'"[iv] The inflatable rafts are full of paying guests and their gear: enormous coolers filled with food, tents, portable stoves, changes of clothes. A special boat goes ahead of the group so that when the expedition arrives at its camp for the night, a gourmet dinner is ready and waiting, and the guests' tents are already set up, with mints on their pillows. In the "radically material encounter" the body grows wings, its tongue flaps or it drips, someone moans about the "delicate balance" of standing on two feet. Guides expand into larger guides; on their days off they play tug-of-war. Walking came before talking in history, if history were a line. But what of flying. Next the sun comes out. The patterns of wings pick up their story in the middle. Guests complain to guides about the weather, as though there were a thermostat on the canyon wall, and someone should twist it.

Matter: source of feeling or emotion.

Close up, the map dissolves into its details, unreadable. EPISODE. We hear cadences in motors gunning and releasing, the speech of two locals outside the window, and certain deformities of tissue. I am feeling so very put-upon, so striped. I remember you mentioned some plans for a founding, but not where you intended to put City Hall. Without you I am intimately fingering Isabella's limbs; though I'm not Land—not really—she is such a Body, so strong and sunburned. She freezes and sweats, tires from gravity's resistance, is nourished by oxygen and sandwiches. I watch her sleeping and trace her hairline. Today I saw the rhythm of walking written on her. She lifts her leg over mine, sighing. Today she told me she was fatigued by the idea of species, and that a succession of trading posts, with their battery-powered headlamps and high-performance fabrics, has made her more tender.

I want to smother her in a way, but then she would only cross me faster.

Circle: fallacious reasoning in which something to be demonstrated is covertly assumed.

(Will you draw up some sort of map to go with this?)

From our observations. Towns engender roads and are engendered by them. A town, brought into being because of a mineral deposit, a bend in a river, or a prosperous homestead, will put out road-veins in order to draw in its lifeblood, population. Where two of these veins meet, in the middle of nothingness, another town may spring up.

There is a trend for converting railroad stations into county historical museums. Inside, historical displays picture the growth of the town. The poetry of this is that the railroad long ago birthed the town and sketched its body. Near the railroad station is downtown. Often called the heart of the town, really it is the face, its window-eyes and trapped speech, words frozen on awnings. And spreading outwards from this central, public presentation: the neighborhoods of houses (arms and legs, utilitarian and, to a degree, individually dispensable), industry (the bowels, taking in ore-food, pumping gasses and black, oily waste), parks (lungs), waterways and railroads (the genitals, irrigated and private, usually not touched).

A town expands from simply a dot on the map, to a grid of streets, to actual streets traveled in an order. Where the built town itself has more memory embedded, the traveler will take away more memory of her own, of hesitant navigation, of rounded or obtuse landmarks, of odd sets of stairs leading off into tiny, useless courtyards. From a grid, she takes corners. Meanwhile, soil underneath.

Form: to take on a definite form, shape, or arrangement.

I am larger all the time, and Isabella keeps finding new corners of me. EPISODE. She puts her nose in my hair and hears small animals making *chuck* and *click* sounds. Where grass meets her knees, she will rub later with her fingernails, or she squints at a faraway horizon of thigh. She tends my wounds where she can. It is a world where certain animals, even some cold-blooded, have calls we hear as human laughter.

I am hemorrhaging intention, and this frightens her. I intend to throw off the leather ties on my flanks. I intend to purify my fluids. I intend to eliminate the space between essence and skin. I intend to put temperature right and to reinstate the extinct. I intend to erase the claw-marks.

Form: to model by instruction and discipline.

The path—gregarious, attractive—shows what is possible for the body to do, has already done, will do again. Each path is a city. The lack of a path is different, an invitation. Pioneers find space an invitation; pilgrims find it an attraction. Full-hearted way through the weeds. Versus porous. What implies motion means time as a line or a circumference, i.e. maps' edges will touch if stretched deep enough. In eating, the body absorbs the land. In travel, the land absorbs the body, but also speech issues itself out. "I had come to be aware of [the place] as one is aware of one's body; it was present to me whether I thought of it or not."[lvi] And there is desire, another blending. A place can be the most complete object of desire; what is for sale is inherently attractive. An obvious liminality, the mouth: eating is descriptive and speaking is inscriptive. "The center, then, is pre-eminently the zone of the sacred, the zone of absolute reality."[lvii]

Form: pattern, schema.

Isabella decides that I as Land am insufferable. She leaves me again. Rearrangement. Of course she cannot vacate entirely, but she puts herself in vinyl rooms. This tingling along the outside of her legs will pleasantly persist whether or not she can feel the outside temperature. She can still put electricity to work in cooking and bathing. Never mind that she learned all this from me before we took on labels; never mind that I taught her how to read a compass. Why am I always so drawn to her sentences, as though she makes a purer line than I can? Her many voyages and her knack with horses are too large in my mind. I have five senses of my own.

She writes: "Here and there the lawns are so smooth, the trees so artistically grouped, a lake makes such an artistic foreground, or a waterfall comes tumbling down with such an apparent feeling for the picturesque, that I am almost angry with Nature for her close imitation of art."[lviii]

Because she is spiteful, she calls you, Machine, and asks you to drive me. I suppose it is only right, only balanced, for the pair of us to convene; and it's true that your vocabulary adds dimension to our pages. I will not hold a grudge, but I will monitor your speed very, very closely. You tell me the crucial thing is to read _____. You lubricate me with your version of the future, the two of us trundling into a burnished memory. You will teach me to recite. First: "The snow isn't beautiful; we see it every day." Then: "_____."

Matter: something written or printed.

Notes on Relations of Machine and Land

The picturesque. A liminal space between land and machine, in that the machine of artmaking arranges and influences and reflects the appearance of the land. Our gardens imitate our wilderness which is then reshaped to look like a garden; our landscape paintings idealize nature which is then held to the painter's standards of composition and human accessibility. We walk through our paintings, then paint images of what we have seen on our walks. The land layered with paint.

The sublime. Case study: In Arches National Park, red sandstone forms fantastical shapes, including enormous archways. The empty space under an arch is full of meaning to the local tourist economy, so some arches are artificially supported to prevent their eventual, natural collapse.

The dead ringer.

The edifying. "The marquis de Giarardin...buried Rosseau on an isle of poplars there and established a pilgrimage for the sentimental devotees who came to pay tribute. It included an itinerary that instructed the visitor not only how to walk through the garden toward the tomb but how to feel."[lix] Park ranger word-processing at dusk: "The asphalt path just across the bridge leads back to your car. As you return to the parking lot, walk slowly and reflect on what you have seen."

Circle: a balcony or tier of seats in a theater.

You and I are walking through a field, remembering it. EPISODE. In my mind are hundreds of photographs of arrows, perhaps taken here, perhaps not. In any case, I look up and see remnants of their sure heads and loyal tails everywhere. Stubs of cornstalks are pointing this way and that, pale and bright against the mud, like an alphabet that hasn't yet been assigned sounds. Green fades over blue. Dissolving arrows are drawn on sides of barns, trunks of trees, the text on a passing truck. Powerlines along the side of the road lead to town. This is what I miss.

As you walk you are reading from a history of this township, saying aloud certain phrases. "Excellent climate," "_____," "broke ground," "_____," "site of this skirmish," "_____," "subdivided among his heirs," "_____," "tremendous resolve."

I feel this is disrespectful but you assure me it's harmless. "See?" you say, "We're almost there." I call you trigger-happy and you call me shapeless. What I will remember of this is the image of you with your back to a long line of deer, silently running south. What you will remember is the crooked road sign reading "_____: 57 miles."

Form: the resting place of a hare.

(more notes — Machine & Land)

The primary. From Ingalls Wilder: A little wagon, filled with a hopeful family, trundles into a sea of grass. This simple image (blue sky, green prairie, like a minimalist painting articulated only by this one enterprising dot in the center, the wagon a pin holding sky and earth together) is enough to serve as primary narrative.

The focal.

The ritualistic. Tourists take photos to record their experience. But if this were the only reason for images, they would leave the photography to the professionals and simply buy postcards. The other reasons are to prove their own arrival and to mark the moment of that arrival so the pilgrims realize they have made it. They arrange themselves into a frontal plane, ignore their surroundings and focus on the machine that will later prove their presence in those surroundings.

The aspirational. "'With two oceans washing our shores, commercial wealth is ours and imagination can hardly conceive the greatness, the grandeur, the power that await us,' the Virginian boomed."[ix] (Horn, 1974)

Matter: mail.

You and I are looking at contemporary postcards from the collection of a most kind woman, Miss Etta Buford of Cody, Wyo. EPISODE. The first one: A "porch." Cars reflected in windows. Park reflected also with its archways built of antlers, collected by Boy Scouts. Detailed and shiny. On the square in Cody, The Gap, Store #6489.

Isabella had written us with an account of a short journey on which she found a mountain pass by asking a string of settlers along her way, mapless, on a rented pony. It puts me in mind of Laura, my old companion. We used to walk through creeks together, scuffing uniform brown scum with bare feet, tugging at overhanging seedheads and what we called "vines." These sometimes put tiny splinters into our fingers. Still, we felt hopeful and clean.

Because the postcard is nearly identical to one you bought in Cody some years earlier, you take it as evidence that our journey will come to a grand conclusion. I picture Isabella and Laura standing in the town square, squinting at cars. "No," you say, "it will be a moment of realization, a feeling of openness and completeness."

Postcards cover the table where we sit, their reds and blues clashing.

Circle: circulate.

> a few more notes; does each pg. need its own title? I'm too tired right now...

The instructive.

The industrial. Description becomes inscription when liminality becomes reproducible.

The nostalgic. We trace lines of anticipation all over the continent. Commercials for places may be more appealing than the places themselves. There is longing not just for the land, but for earlier forms of tourism. The ladies in their hoop skirts, posing on the cliffs under parasols, having ridden in on mules.

The legible. "[Villagers] are wayworn by the travel that goes by and over them, without traveling themselves."[lxi] Tourism writes the story and tourists only read it. Of course they do not go knocking on strangers' doors, asking for bread and water. "We *still* have not, in any meaningful way, arrived in America."[lxii]

Line: a circle of latitude or longitude on a map.

Another postcard shows the backside of a grandstand, one C large and red on the white, standing for Cody Nite Rodeo. EPISODE. Also a painted bronco, bucking, rider with boots splayed and chaps a-flying, ten-gallon, spurs, dungareed pardners leaning on the stylized fence behind. Angles of stadium, of sunset, of actual man looking at hill, a ramp for the handicapped, dumpster for everyone. "Section E & F" and white lines for driving.

I feel like I want to smell the dry grass under the boots, and follow the tracks of pickups back into town as they loop behind ranch houses and aboveground swimming pools. But when I picture doing this I see, as if in clear memory, your hovering shadow in the corner of my vision, like a museum guard.

You pull a different postcard, one covered in text, and read the whole thing to me: "Snake River Kayak & Canoe School. Mangis Fishing Guide Service. Chuckwagon Supper and Western Show. Grand Teton National Park Activities. Exum Mountain Guides. Horseback Riding At Its Best. Dornan's Original Chuck Wagon. Yellowstone Bear World. Teton Mountain Bike Tours. Unguided Horse & Raft Rentals. Wildlife Expeditions. Yippy I-O Candy Co. Cowboy Village Resort. The Virginian Lodge. The Hatchet. Flat Creek Motel. Fine Art That Depicts Wildlife. Teton Club. Old Time Photo Studio. The Edge Sports."

(more)

The serviceable. Mnemonic palace: medieval technique for memorizing long texts, in which each detail of the narrative is mentally attached to a feature of an imagined palace, thus allowing one to recite the text by wandering through the building. A tourist destination is like a mnemonic palace that exists physically, in the world. Whereas the mental confection can be made to remain as it was originally built, reliably clutching its narrative, a three-dimensional place that exists on the earth is always in flux. The narrative wants to mutate along with its physical embodiment.

The substantive. "Any meaningful act performed by archaic man, any real act, i.e., any repetition of an archetypal gesture, suspends duration, abolishes profane time, and participates in mythical time."[lxiii] (Eliade.)

The amiss. Nothing really changes when we watch a mock gunfight or put on a ten-gallon hat. (However, the past remains quite relevant; in the West we are still fighting over water.) If nostalgia is Arcadian, a wish for what has been lost, tourism's sentiments are a false front that affirm the superiority of progress. They are thus Utopian.

The devout.

Line: equator.

Even after we return the cards to Miss Buford and continue on our way, the journey is tense. EPISODE. I edit my speech as it leaves my mouth and secretly throw small items of yours into the trash: receipts, keys. But you seem not to notice. Your new habit each morning—to read every word you can find in our luggage, in the glove box, on billboards in your view. You do this with an air of hunger, and file our maps alphabetically in a metal box. We have become faintly antagonistic in our talk, especially in the afternoons when the road takes on the feeling of conveyor belt, shuttling us in our half-sleep to some wider vista. "_____," you will say, as though alluding to my faults as a navigator. I answer with vaguely stormy intimations.

You always were attentive, if worriedly, to Isabella, but with me you are nearly imperious. I am sorry I lack her smooth arms and loping gait; I am unfocused, yes, and harder to find at the end of a stroll. I have been late to a rendezvous or two. And I have dripped water on your inked words.

We do agree in bafflement at towns called Bliss, or Kill Buck. There must be a high place to see from. Cutting, Beaver Dams, Lock Berlin; how people decided to stop or to rest, then go; building on which arm of which creek. Handwriting is never twice the same, much less gridded. Questa. Daretown. Bridgeton. Hopewell, Wing, Cogswell, Edgeley. Near a border, Wheelock. We know if Isabella were here she would look through narrow eyes at the folds of hills.

She writes us again: "The shallow Platte, shriveled into a narrow stream with a shingly bed six times too large for it, and fringed by shriveled cotton-wood, wound along by Denver, and two miles up its course I saw a great sandstorm, which in a few minutes covered the city, blotting it out with a dense brown cloud."[lxiv]

So we go and find her on the river.

Circle: a circle formed on the surface of a sphere by the intersection of a plane that passes through it.

(and the last of these, finally)

The schematic. Grid system is a container that encloses distance by marking it, shutting out a sense of vastness. Under the grid, swelling its terms, are the ragged scrawled fingers of creeks and rivers.

The watchful. If the land is empty, the machine will fill it.

The enterprising. "This huge gash is gauged through hills, the rubble from which of course you then use to fill in the valleys so that the roads create this whole new geological feature that is 100 miles long and much the same level from one end to the other…If the whole surface of the earth is mappable then in a sense the line of sight becomes a line of force."[lxv]

The geometric. A river has a hidden belowness; it is the closest reading of the landscape, always by gravity, minutely down. When water disrupts a grid, it opens the way for unarticulated space to re-enter—the wild space that existed in paintings before the picture plane was conceived as a window onto a perspectival space. When we use a grid to map actual land, we bring wildness under control as resource, as background, as setting for our actions.

The unseen.

The splintered. A map, claiming truthfulness, makes a journey episodic.

We all sit, facing each other, in a field behind a gas station. CLOSING. We put our round heads together; we decay and cry over our faded ambitions. We drop our costumes; we drop our names. We palm each other's shoulders. In a dense mass of trees, sentences trickle away. In a field of girdled trees they might bake all morning. Isabella draws the two of us in and begins a speech.

"We are defeated by distance. Our manifesto has proven impossible to enact. We have gotten nowhere. Our book which set out to be enclosed will now remain unfinished. We were pilgrims after all; pioneering eludes us. We meant to face home but got turned around, spoiled, and changed states. We saw creation and were repulsed. Water fell from our fingers, from our wheel-well, from our repeated accounts. We drowned in contemplation; we saw the pollution of the view with clearer eyes than we could bear. The lines of our route became refracted. We suspected a recurrence under every straight shot. We could not adequately separate our eras. We lost track of what was inside or outside any frame; things on opposite sides of a window became more alike, and names blinded us. We gazed at each other across a divide; we smothered each other with speech. We looked down at a map and saw it moving. We turned away all offers and still purchased thousands. We lost track of our own verbs. We triangulated our location and then it slid downhill. We looked for clearings and could not escape them. We must ritualize our suspicion that all lines eventually converge. We slept in machines; we breathed outside air; we were distracted from movement by the view. Our roles made fractious cartoons of us. We attempted to map a triangle one side at a time, and found it collapsed. We tried to tease out a burr and embedded it more deeply. We spit on grids that were thousands of townships in size. We guessed wrongly that we could push our episodes down into a story. Having been initiated into circularity, we must make a final gesture in harmony with the liminalities that have swallowed us."

Given our need for a summary rite, I suggest turning in place, running our eyes over treelines.

But you, reader: you take a piece of paper and a pen, and you walk away—you walk as we keep up our elegy, our reminiscence and declaration,

our words floating near and away:

> [Notes on the Circular]
> (... or something like that. This is where it all comes together, but we have some serious hashing out to do before we write this up. As you'll see below.)

First you write down
a scent, here:

>	—slept among dunes and yellow flowers—someone was up there carving decorative touches on the eaves. It was a cold and pine-scented night. Lathe-bound, ruddy—

Then the feel of the ground,
how hard or soft:

>	—the newels tumbled down. Change is now electrified. A shadow obliterates some grasses. "A folded form—

Then three things you see,
all of similar size:

>	is like a drawstring bag; opposite fabrics touch at the top, at the bottom they perfectly meet. Porous rock, big holes, made into a wall—

>	—a motel in front of the mountain, a car, a shop window full of antlers and feathers, phonelines, small RV, the bank, in front of the mountain—

Then a birdcall you hear:

     —have admired you Isabella for decades, aching
     decades, but all the points are smoothing down—

Then the relative sunniness:

     —no polygon, no purposeful role or beehive.
     Change is now electrified. A kind of alphabet
       with light and dark versions. A road

Then whether you are facing
downhill or up:

     is a long thin clearing. A clearing has edges
     between empty and full, and the road's shoulder
          is a borderland—

Then something right at your
feet:

     —that all generality embeds in what angle. That
     I made it back before the rain. They call it a pass—

     —Thirty thousand miles in a summer. Wood
     became scarce; our heavy skirts
       keep us from offering more—

Then the tallest thing
you can see:

     —Plains, plains everywhere, generally level, but
     elsewhere rolling in long undulations, like the
     waves of a sea which had fallen asleep—

Then, if you hear any
traffic, its tone:

       —one could gallop all over them—

Then the sound of your
steps:

> Trees part in the middle, obvious slopes are
> streaked. Change is now electrified. A lake
> named after a woman meets its shores
> half-worriedly—

Then the temperature of the air
in your nostrils:

> —allness of the allness of the bowl on the rim
> of the painted waterfall scene. Well-worn: the red
> bark, dark needles, the illusion sky. A small brown
> sign gave our elevation. Trunks rode back along
> the slopes, holding rocks in roots—

Then whether gates or fences
are in view:

> Isabella, you palm tiny trees, every so often
> a curb breaks on intersection—
>
> You count out: *2 pair fine blue stockings, 1 pair
> fine red stockings, 4 white handkerchiefs,
> 2 speckled handkerchiefs*…

Then how many people
are visible:

> —She abandons me for a lean-to.
> I recreate on deep blue glass.
>
> The truth is each place seems more meaningful
> when it is part of an arrangement.

Then how many cars
are visible:

> Change is now electrified. "We write a text
> to find our place in English, we cut down trees
> to find our place on the map." A dozen keyed
> mailboxes, gabled summer house, plastic bear.

>			The heat of this, the rainbow on the side
>				of the store. It all leans a little.—

Then the song in your
head:

>			—the lovely hue of dusk on a picnic table
>		was so menacing that food became like ash.—

Then how many houses
are visible:

>				—a place robbed of rain is inward,
>			uninterested. *The scythe, which only slowly
>								changed.*
>
>			*Settlers sought to reproduce houses they had
>			They dared neither fish nor hunt nor farm.
>				A stockpile of pikes, swords—*

Then whether any other person
is walking your direction:

>			—Tight lines of citrus, a dirt road, a highway.
>			Flat-bottom punctuation, darker vegetated ridge.
>			Streaks of lime-green on forest. Someone squeezed
>				in seven more trees there, and a ditch of dark.

Then something only partially
visible:

>				Living right by the canal is clouds at breakfast,
>									twice as many paths.

Then the character
of the wind:

>			"If the circle is a wheel, it works against the ground
>				to become a line. Linear travel is for destination.
>				If the circle is a meander, it wanders over the

>   ground and its line turns congenially back on itself.
>   Circular travel is for contemplation."

Then whether you
are hungry:

> —walking a very large circle, or downstream, a line
>   is a line is peeling. Skin of grass or of moment.
> Light folds through water over folded rock, eroding.
>   Cars wait at a light, heading off-camera.

Then the last animal
you saw:

> —A journey is a clearing in time—

Then how seasonable
the weather:

> —Shingles rotted in the shade. A tree close by
>   might fall so you girdle it. Your sweaty ax breaks.
>   The root of *cultivation, culture* and *cult* meaning
>   both "to revolve" and "to dwell."
>   A blur on near weeds.

Then the most inviting
spot in view:

> —in the morning this would be tawny and blue,
>   with moss at the edge. See you taking on aspects of
>   each other's faces; see you loping down her sides.
>   She is sky-blue, baby-blue.
>   A desperate bit of shelter
>   made of paint and sand.—

Then the part of the view
you're ignoring:

> The circumference swallows itself and I dive into
> the center of you and the center of you and
> there's nothing different here
> except the people are gone.

Then the direction of the spot
you consider your origin:

> —Pockets of green comb the wind.

> "Even places dreamed all at once, platted in an
> afternoon on the prairie, are signatures, organic,
> much deeper than their grids, which swell with
> weeds and memory."

Then something that is moving:

> The curving lines of wheat, watered
> by a center-pivot irrigator.

Then you stand in fescue.

You gaze straight along a line
in front of you.

You write on your sheet of paper,
How is travel a folded form?

You drop it at your feet.

Acknowledgments

Grateful acknowledgment to the readers and encouragers: Thalia Field, Kate Schapira, Jen Tynes, Tyler Carter, Susan Scarlata, Kelli Auerbach, Lori Anderson Moseman, Katie Yates, Melanie Noel, Keith Waldrop, Rosmarie Waldrop, Martha Collins, Pam Alexander, Ed Smallfield, Michael Gizzi.

Thank you to Ruth Thompson and Don Mitchell for the attention and care they have given this book.

Love and gratitude to John.

About the Author

Erika Howsare lives in rural Virginia, where she mothers full-time and works as a journalist. With Kate Schapira, she wrote a book-length poetic meditation on waste, called *FILL: A Collection*, published by Trembling Pillow Press in 2016. She was a co-editor at Horse Less Press for 11 years and has published three chapbooks; a fourth, *Spinning Pins*, is forthcoming from Magnificent Field in 2018. Her prose appears in *Taproot* and online at The Millions and The Rumpus. Previous projects included a performative multimedia walk across Rhode Island and a literary reenactment of the Lewis and Clark expedition.

Endnotes

i. Isabella L. Bird, *A Lady's Life in the Rocky Mountains* (Norman, OK: University of Oklahoma Press, 1960), 20.
ii. Henry David Thoreau, *Walking: A Little Book of Wisdom* (San Francisco: HarperCollins, 1994), 3.
iii. Daniel J. Boorstin, intro to ibid, xvi-xvii.
iv. Bird, 37.
v. Ibid, 102.
vi. Theodore H. Hittell, "The Continent is Joined" in Tony Hillerman, *The Best of the West: An Anthology of Classic Writing from the American West* (New York: HarperCollins, 1991), 424.
vii. Bird, 31.
viii. *Observer-Reporter*, Washington (PA), Feb. 22, 2004.
ix. Bird, 24.
x. Mircea Eliade, *Cosmos and History: The Myth of the Eternal Return* (New York: Harper & Row, 1959), 73.
xi. Susan Howe, *The Birth-mark: unsettling the wilderness in American literary history* (Hanover, NH: Wesleyan University Press, 1993), 58.
xii. Eliade, 19. Full quote: "The act of foundation at the same time repeats the cosmogonic act, for to 'secure' the snake's head, to drive the peg into it, is to imitate the primordial gesture…Indra comes upon Vrtra undivided…the hurling of the lightning and the decapitation are equivalent to the act of Creation, with passage from the nonmanifested to the manifested, from the formless to the formed."
xiii. Thoreau, "Cape Cod", quoted in Ronald P. Morrison, "Wilderness and Clearing: Thoreau, Heidegger, and the Poetic", *Interdisciplinary Studies in Literature and Environment* 10, Issue 1 (Jan. 1, 2003), 155.
xiv. Eliade, 54.
xv. Lucy R. Lippard, *The Lure of the Local: Senses of Place in a Multicentered Society* (New York: The New Press, 1997), 42.
xvi. Huston Horn/Editors of Time-Life Books, *The Pioneers* (Alexandria, VA: Time-Life Books, 1974), 173.

[xvii] "Thus the bridge does not first come to a location to stand in it; rather, a location comes into existence only by virtue of the bridge." Martin Heidegger, in "Building Dwelling Thinking," quoted in Morrison, 155.

[xviii] Stephanie Strickland, "Retuning Time and Space in Digital Media." Talk at Brown University, Providence, RI, Feb. 18, 2004.

[xix] Eliade, 11.

[xx] Julian Smith, *Moon Handbooks: Virginia* (Emeryville, CA: Avalon Travel Publishing, 2002), 31.

[xxi] Rebecca Solnit, *As Eve Said to the Serpent: On Landscape, Gender, and Art* (Athens, GA: University of Georgia Press, 2001), 185.

[xxii] Bird, 80.

[xxiii] Lippard, 132.

[xxiv] Bird, 34.

[xxv] Bird, 48.

[xxvi] Ibid, 48.

[xxvii] J.C. Ruppenthal, quoted in Joanna L. Stratton, *Pioneer Women: Voices from the Kansas Frontier* (New York: Simon & Schuster, 1981), 61.

[xxviii] Thoreau, 30.

[xxix] Solnit, 156.

[xxx] Bird, 44.

[xxxi] Ibid, 44.

[xxxii] Ian Austen, "Pictures, With Map and Pushpin Included," New York Times, Nov. 2, 2006.

[xxxiii] *Moon Metro: Washington, D.C.* (Emeryville, CA: Avalon Travel Publishing, 2002), map 2.

[xxxiv] Horn, 116.

[xxxv] Bird, 54.

[xxxvi] Martin Heidegger, *Poetry, Language, Thought* (New York: Harper and Row, 1971), 222.

[xxxvii] Solnit, 152.

[xxxviii] Ann-Marie Brown, *California Waterfalls* (Emeryville, CA: Avalon Travel, 2004).

[xxxix] Bird, 24.

xl	Cole Swensen, *Noon* (Los Angeles: Sun & Moon Press, 1997), 11.
xli	Henry David Thoreau, *Walden: Or, Life in the Woods*, (T.Y. Crowell, 1899), 191.
xlii	John Berger, *Ways of Seeing* (London: British Broadcasting Corporation, 1972), 99.
xliii	Thoreau, *Walden*, 122.
xliv	Swensen, 11.
xlv	Bird, 3.
xlvi	Ibid, 23.
xlvii	Austin, 214.
xlviii	Solnit, *Wanderlust* (New York: Viking, 2000), 258.
xlix	Bird, 77.
l	Wendell Berry, *The Art of the Commonplace: The Agrarian Essays of Wendell Berry* (Emeryville, CA: Shoemaker & Hoard, 2002), 12.
li	Bird, 142.
lii	Solnit, *Wanderlust*, 50.
liii	Thoreau, 39.
liv	Yi-Fu Tuan, *Space and Place: The Perspective of Experience* (Minneapolis: University of Minnesota Press, 1977), 110.
lv	Horn, 69.
lvi	Berry, 5.
lvii	Eliade, 17.
lviii	Bird, 106.
lix	Solnit, *Wanderlust*, 22.
lx	Horn, 43.
lxi	Thoreau, 14.
lxii	Berry, 11.
lxiii	Eliade, 36.
lxiv	Bird, 137.
lxv	McKenzie Wark (with John Kinsella), "Landfill," *CHAIN* 9 (2002): 157.
lxvi	Mary Austin, "The American Rhythm," *NO: A Journal of the Arts* 2 (2003): 211.

CPSIA information can be obtained
at www.ICGtesting.com
Printed in the USA
BVHW04s0329290518
517467BV00002B/48/P